Mouse's Night Before Christmas

Mouse's Night Before Christmas

Tracey Corderoy

Sarah Massini

nosy crow

'Twas the night before Christmas,
when all through the house
not a creature was stirring,
not even a mouse.

That is how the tale started,
the one that you know.
But I'll tell you a secret –
it **wasn't** quite so.
Because if you look closer,
you might see a door
at the foot of the grandfather clock,
near the floor.
And you'll see that it's open . . .

. . . and look! A small nose,
and two twinkly black eyes,
and some tiny pink toes.

On that night before Christmas,
dear reader, you see
there was one little mouse
as awake as could be.

And he peeped at the Christmas tree there in the hall.
It had candles, and tinsel, and quite best of all . . .
"Lots of presents!" he gasped. Then the mouse shook his head.
"If I just had a friend to give gifts to . . ." he said.

"Oh, but look!" exclaimed Mouse, how excited to see
the most beautiful star at the top of the tree.
He had **heard** stars gave wishes! But could it be true?
And he wondered if plain little mice might wish too . . .

He decided to try it, in case they just might,
so he whispered his tiny wish into the night.

But then out on the lawn
there arose such a clatter,
that he scurried outside
to see what was the matter . . .

As he peeped round a plant pot, Mouse let out a cry –
"Gosh, it's Santa and so many reindeer. Oh my!"

"What a storm!" Santa shivered. "I'm sorry to say
that I think, my dear Rudolph, we've quite lost our way!"

Then he checked to make sure all his reindeer were there,
as the snow whirled about in the frosty night air.

"There's Dasher, there's Dancer,
there's Prancer, and Vixen.
And Comet, and Cupid,
and Donner, and Blitzen.
And Rudolph of course!
And there's – wait . . .

. . . who are you?"

"I'm just Mouse," blushed the mouse. "Oh . . . um, how do you do?"
"Was it your wish I heard?" Santa's eyes twinkled bright.
"Why, I did make a wish!" nodded Mouse with delight.

Then he squeaked, "But you're lost! So the good girls and boys,
who are tucked up and sleeping, won't get any toys!"

For a moment Mouse thought, then he suddenly cried,
"I know just what to do – please take me as your guide.
I go out quite a lot when I'm lonely, you see,
so if anyone knows their way round, well – it's me."

With a smile, Santa whisked him up onto the sleigh,
and before Mouse could blink, they were up and away!

As the moon brightly shone and the snow drifted down,
little Mouse led the way through the streets of the town.

Oh, what fun he had helping to carry the toys
and then fill up the stockings of good girls and boys.

He was quiet, and careful, and ever so neat –
quite the best little helper that Santa could meet!

When their work was all done, Santa landed and said,
"I must leave you now, Mouse, and fly home to my bed."

"Must you go?" whispered Mouse, blinking back a small tear.
"It was just . . . just so friendly to have someone here."

As the snow iced the rooftops all sparkly and white,
"I'll be back," Santa promised, "next Christmas Eve night.
But till then, Mouse – your wish – I remembered, you know."
And he held out a box with a lovely red bow.

Mouse unwrapped it at once.
"Oh!" The skates were so sweet.
But why four when he only had two tiny feet?

"That's not all!" Santa smiled. "It will soon become clear
if you follow this map – look, the path is marked here."

"Will the path lead the way to my wish?" the mouse cried.
Santa winked. "Why not see for yourself?" he replied.

With a bright, "Ho, ho, ho!"
Santa called from his sleigh,
"Very soon, little Mouse,
it will be Christmas Day!"

And then —

OOOOsh

— he was off through the starry night sky,
as the mouse far below waved a final goodbye.

So Mouse followed the path,

which went up
and went down.

Why, it seemed to be taking him all over town!

Then it led to the park

and at last to a tree.
And then up on a snowy branch,
what should Mouse see . . .

. . . but a small, fluffy bird with his eyes big and wide.
"Oh, could you be the friend that I wished for?" Bird cried.

"For a **friend**?" exclaimed Mouse.
"But I wished for that too!"
Then he held up the skates,

"Happy Christmas to you!"

So, dear reader, you see on that night long ago,
Mouse was **not** in his clock but outside in the snow!

And he skated with Bird till the dark sky turned blue,
two new friends with just **one** Christmas wish . . .

that came true.

For Laetitia, with love . . . T.C.

For Manda – may all your Christmases be merry – S.M.

First published 2019 by Nosy Crow Ltd
The Crow's Nest, 14 Baden Place
Crosby Row, London SE1 1YW
www.nosycrow.com

ISBN 978 1 78800 540 1 (HB)
ISBN 978 1 78800 544 9 (PB)

Nosy Crow and associated logos are trademarks
and/or registered trademarks of Nosy Crow Ltd

Text © Tracey Corderoy 2019
Illustrations © Sarah Massini 2019

The right of Tracey Corderoy to be identified as the author and
Sarah Massini to be identified as the illustrator of this work has been asserted.

A CIP catalogue record for this book is available from the British Library.

Printed in China
Papers used by Nosy Crow are made from wood grown in
sustainable forests.

10 9 8 7 6 5 4 3 2 1 (HB)
10 9 8 7 6 5 4 3 2 1 (PB)